Missy:

Happy Birthday (81)

Much love,
Mandy (X)

THE GLASS SLIPPER
Charles Perrault's Tales of Times Past

THE GLASS SLIPPER

Charles Perrault's Tales of Times Past

Translated by John Bierhorst

Illustrated by Mitchell Miller

Four Winds Press   New York

Library of Congress Cataloging in Publication Data

Perrault, Charles, 1628–1703/The glass slipper.

Translation of Contes.
Summary/A modern translation of "Sleeping Beauty,"
"Puss in Boots," "Little Red Riding Hood," and "Cinderella."
1. Fairy tales, French. [1. Fairy tales.   2. Folklore—France]
I. Bierhorst, John.   II. Miller, Mitchell, 1947–   III. Title.
PZ8.P426Gl   1980   398.2   80-66243
ISBN 0-590-07603-5

Published by Four Winds Press
A division of Scholastic Inc., New York, N.Y.
Text copyright © 1981 by John Bierhorst
Illustrations copyright © 1981 by Mitchell Miller
All rights reserved/Printed in the United States of America
Library of Congress Catalog Card Number: 80-66243
Designed by Jane Byers Bierhorst
1   2   3   4   5   85   84   83   82   81

A limited edition of this book has
been privately printed.

Frontispiece/A reinterpretation by
Mitchell Miller of the frontispiece by
Clouzier in the first edition (January 1697)
of Perrault's *Contes du temps passé*.

Contents

THE GLASS SLIPPER
Charles Perrault's Tales of Times Past

The Sleeping Beauty

Once upon a time there lived a king and a queen who were extremely worried that they had no children, so worried it can't be described. They went to all the watering places. Vows, pilgrimages, prayers, they tried everything. But it was no use. At last, however, the queen became pregnant and gave birth to a girl.

They had a beautiful christening, and all the fairies that could be found in the land were presented to the little princess as godmothers (there were seven). With each one making a wish for the child, as was the custom with fairies in those days, the princess would have every imaginable perfection.

When the christening cere-monies were over, the guests returned to the king's palace, where a great banquet was held for the fairies. Each one had a magnificent dinner service with a spoon, a fork, and a knife of pure gold, studded with diamonds and rubies, in a solid gold case. But just as they were about to sit at the table an old fairy appeared who had not been invited. She had not left her tower in more than fifty years, and every-body had thought she was dead, or bewitched.

At the king's command they set a place for her. But it was impossible to give her a solid gold dinnerware case like the others, because they had only had seven made, one for each of the seven fairies. The old fairy felt slighted and muttered a few threats between her teeth. One of the young fairies sitting next to her overheard this and, suspecting she might make a bad wish for the little princess, went and hid behind a tapestry as soon as they had all left the table, so that she could be the last to speak. In this way, as best she could, she would make up for whatever harm the old fairy might do.

Meanwhile the fairies began to make their wishes for the princess. The youngest wished that she would be the most beautiful creature in the world, the next youngest that she would have the wit of an angel, the third that she would be wonderfully graceful in all her actions, the fourth that she would be a perfect dancer, the fifth that she would sing like a nightingale, and the sixth that she would play all sorts of instruments to the utmost perfection.

The old fairy's turn had come. Her head shaking more with spite than with age, she declared that the princess would prick her hand on a spindle, and from this she would die.

The terrible wish made everyone shudder, and no one could keep from crying. Just at that moment the young fairy came out from behind the tapestry and pronounced these words in a loud voice:

"Set your minds at rest, O king and O queen! Your daughter will not die. It is true, I haven't the power to completely unmake what my elder has done. The princess will prick her hand on a spindle. But instead of dying, she will merely fall into a deep sleep lasting a hundred years, and then a king's son will come to awaken her."

Hoping to avoid the misfortune predicted by the old fairy, the king sent out an order forbidding anyone to spin, or to have

a spindle in the house, on pain of death.

After fifteen or sixteen years, the king and queen having gone off to one of their country estates, it came about that the young princess, roaming through the castle one day and climbing from room to room, reached the top of a tower, and there in a small garret, alone, was an old woman spinning. This woman had never heard of the king's prohibition against using a spindle.

"What are you doing there, good woman?" said the princess.

"I'm spinning, my pretty child," answered the old woman, not realizing who the girl was.

"Oh, how nice that looks!" said the princess. "How do you do it? Here, let me see if I can do as well."

Eager as she was, and being a little careless—and for the reason moreover that the fairies had decreed it must be so—no sooner had she taken the spindle than she pricked her hand and fell unconscious. Greatly distressed, the old woman cried out for help. People came from all directions. They threw water in the princess's face, they loosened her lacings, they patted her with their hands, they rubbed her temples with Queen of Hungary's water, but nothing would revive her.

Then the king, who had returned to the palace and had immediately climbed upstairs upon hearing the noise, remembered the fairies' prediction. Assuming that this is what must have happened, inasmuch as the fairies had said it would, he had the princess placed in the most beautiful apartment in the palace on a bed embroidered with gold and silver.

She seemed an angel, so beautiful she was. Her swoon had not taken away the glowing colors from her complexion. Her cheeks were carnation, her lips were like coral. She merely had her eyes closed. And she could be heard breathing gently, which proved that she was not dead. The king commanded that she be allowed to sleep in peace until the time should come for her awakening.

The good fairy who had saved her life by sentencing her to a hundred years' sleep was in the kingdom of Matakin, twelve thousand leagues away, at the time the princess had her accident. But in a moment she was told what had happened by a little dwarf who had seven-league boots (these were the boots that made seven leagues at a single stride). The fairy set out at once and arrived an hour later in a fiery chariot, drawn by dragons.

The king came and offered her his hand as she climbed out of the chariot. She approved of everything he had done. But being possessed of great foresight, she knew that when the princess awakened she would be much distressed all alone in the old castle. So this is what she did.

Except for the king and queen, she touched everyone in the castle with her wand, governesses, maids of honor, ladies in waiting, gentlemen, housemasters, stewards, chefs, scullions, kitchen boys, guards, Switzers, pages, and footmen. She touched all the horses in the stables, and the grooms, and the huge mastiffs in the stable yard, and even little Pouf, the princess's lap dog, who lay beside her on her bed.

As she touched them, they all fell asleep, to awaken only with their mistress, so that they would be ready to serve her when she needed them. Even the spits on the fire, all loaded with partridges and pheasants, slept. And the fire as well. It all happened in a moment. Fairies are not long at their work.

Then the king and the queen, after kissing their dear child without her waking, took leave of the castle and made a proclamation forbidding anyone to go near it. This was not necessary, however, for in a quarter of an hour so many trees, both large and small, and all intertwined with brambles and thorns, had grown up around the park that neither man nor beast could have passed through, and nothing could be seen of the castle except for the tops of its towers, and only from far away. No one doubted that this too was a work of the fairy's art, so that the princess, as she slept, would have nothing to fear from prying eyes.

At the end of a hundred years the son of the king who was reigning at that time—and who belonged to a different family from that of the sleeping princess—was out hunting in those parts and asked what the towers were that he saw rising above a large and very dense wood. People told him whatever they had heard. Some said that it was an old castle haunted by ghosts, others that it was where all the local witches held their sabbath. The most common opinion was that an ogre lived there and that this was where he carried off all the children he caught, so that he could eat them at his leisure without anyone following him, for he alone had the power to pass through the wood.

The prince didn't know which to believe. Then an old peasant spoke up and said, "My prince, over fifty years ago I heard my father say that in that castle there was a princess, the most beautiful in the world, and that she would have to sleep a hundred years and would be awakened by a king's son, for whom she was intended."

Upon hearing this, the young prince was all afire. Without thinking twice, he knew that it was for him to bring this noble adventure to its conclusion, and spurred by love and glory he immediately resolved to see what it was all about.

Scarcely had he started toward the wood than all those tall trees, those brambles, and those thorns parted to let him pass. He walked toward the castle, which he could see at the end of a

great pathway that he now entered, and somewhat to his surprise he saw that not one of his party was able to follow him, for the trees closed behind him as he passed through. Nevertheless he went on. A young prince in love is always brave.

He came to a great forecourt, where all that he saw at first might have chilled him with fear. There was a ghastly silence and a vision of death on all sides—nothing but stretched-out bodies of men and animals, seemingly dead. But he could tell by the Switzers' red noses and flushed faces that they were only sleeping, and the few drops of wine remaining in their cups proved that they had drunk themselves to sleep.

He went through a large court paved with marble, climbed a staircase, and entered the guard room. The guards stood all in a row, their muskets on their shoulders, snoring as loudly as they could. He passed through several rooms filled with gentlemen and ladies, all asleep, some standing, some seated. He entered a chamber all gilded, and there, on a bed with its curtains flung wide, he saw the most beautiful sight he had ever seen: a princess who appeared to be fifteen or sixteen, and whose radiant glow had something shining and holy about it. Trembling and filled with wonder, he approached and knelt beside her.

Now that the magic spell had been broken, the princess awakened, and gazing at him with eyes more tender than would have seemed possible at first sight, she said, "Is it you, my prince? You were long in coming."

Charmed by these words and even more so by the manner in which they were spoken, the prince was at a loss to express his joy and his thankfulness. He assured her that he loved her more than his own self. His words, though plain, were more pleasing that way: short on eloquence, long on love.

It was harder for him than it was for her, and no wonder. She had had time to think about what she would tell him. (Though the story says nothing about this, it seems that the good fairy had given her pleasant dreams during her long sleep.) And so

they talked on, for four hours. And even so they did not say half the things they wanted to say.

Meanwhile the whole palace had awakened with the princess. All were attending to their duties and, as not everyone was in love, they were all dying of hunger. The lady of honor, in as great a hurry as the rest, finally lost her patience and called out to the princess that dinner was served. The prince helped the princess get out of bed. She was fully dressed and magnificently so. But he was careful not to tell her that she was dressed as our grandmothers used to be, with a high-backed ruff, for she was beautiful even so.

They entered a hall of mirrors, and there they dined, served by the princess's housemasters. Violins and oboes played old-fashioned tunes, which were still good even if people no longer played them and hadn't in nearly a hundred years. After dinner, without wasting time, the grand almoner married them in the palace chapel, and the lady of honor drew the bed curtains.

They slept little. The princess hardly needed to. And when morning came the prince left her and returned to the town, where his father was anxiously awaiting him. The prince told him that while out hunting he had lost his way in the forest and had slept in the hut of a charcoal burner, who had given him black bread and cheese to eat.

His father, the king, who was a simple man, believed him. But his mother was not completely persuaded and, seeing that he went hunting almost every day thereafter and always had a ready excuse when he had slept out for two or three nights, she no longer doubted that he was in love.

Indeed, he lived with the princess more than two whole years and had two children by her, of which the first was a daughter, called Dawn, and the second a son—called Day, because he was even more beautiful than his sister.

In order to get the truth out of him, the queen kept telling her son it was time for him to settle down. But he never dared trust her with his secret. He was afraid of her even though he loved her, for she was descended from a line of ogres, and the king had only married her on account of her great wealth.

It was even whispered around the court that she had an ogre's appetite and that whenever she saw little children passing by, it was all she could do to keep from pouncing on them. And so the prince said nothing.

But when the king died, two years later, and he saw that he was now the ruler, he publicly announced his marriage and with great ceremony went to fetch his wife, the queen, at her castle. A magnificent reception was held for her in the principal town, where she made her entrance together with her two children, one at each side.

Some time thereafter, the king went and made war on his neighbor, the emperor Cantalabutte. He left the kingdom to be ruled by his mother, charging her to take good care of his wife and children. He was to be at war for the entire summer, and as soon as he had gone the queen mother sent her daughter-in-law and the children to a country seat, off in the woods, where it would be easier to satisfy her horrible desire. She arrived a few days later, and one evening she said to her steward, "I'll have little Dawn for dinner tomorrow."

"Oh, madame!" said the steward.

"I shall!" she said, and she spoke with the voice of an ogress craving fresh meat. "And I'll have her with sauce Robert."

The poor man, knowing better than to trifle with an ogress, took his long knife and went upstairs to little Dawn's bedroom. She was four years old at the time, and she came with a bound, laughing, and threw her arms around his neck, asking him for a piece of candy. He began to cry. The knife fell from his hand, and he went down to the barnyard and slit the throat of a young lamb and made such a nice sauce for it that his mistress assured him she had never eaten  anything better. At the same time, he had taken little Dawn and had given her to his wife to hide in her quarters at the far end of the kitchen yard.

A week later the wicked queen said to her steward, "I'll have little Day for dinner," and he made no answer, having decided to fool her as he had done before. He went to get little Day and found him with a tiny foil in his hand, fencing with a pet monkey, though he was only three years old. He took him to his wife, who hid him with little Dawn. And in place of little Day he served a very tender young kid, which the ogress thought wonderfully good.

Up to that point everything had gone well. But one evening this wicked queen said to the steward, "I'll have the queen with the same sauce as the children."

At this the poor steward despaired of deceiving her. The young queen was past twenty, not counting the hundred years she had slept. Her skin was quite tough, even if beautiful and fair. How could he find an animal in the barn as tough as this?

In order to save his own life, he resolved to slit the queen's throat, and he went upstairs to her bedroom, intending to get it over with. He worked himself into a frenzy and went into the young queen's room with the dagger in his hand. Nevertheless, he didn't want to take her by surprise, and with great respect he explained to her the order he had received from the queen mother.

"Do your duty," she told him, stretching out her neck. "Carry out the command you've been given. I shall see my children again, my poor children whom I loved so," for they had been carried off without a word and she thought they were dead.

"No, no, madame!" replied the poor steward, filled with

pity. "You will not die. Nor will you fail to see your beloved children again, for they are in my quarters, where I have hidden them. And again I will fool the queen, by having her eat a young doe in your place."

He took her at once to his room and left her there embracing her children and weeping with them, while he went off to dress a doe, which the ogress ate at supper, relishing it as though it had been the young queen. She was well pleased with her cruelty and was prepared to tell her son that mad wolves had eaten his wife and two children.

One evening while prowling around the castle gardens and kitchen quarters as usual, sniffing for fresh meat, she heard little Day crying behind a door. The queen, his mother, was about to whip him for being naughty. She also heard little Dawn, asking that her brother be forgiven. The ogress recognized the voices of the queen and her children and was furious at having been deceived.

The next morning, in a voice so terrible that everyone quivered, she ordered a huge vat brought to the middle of the yard and filled with toads, vipers, snakes, and serpents, so that the queen, the children, the steward, his wife, and his servant girl could all be thrown into it.

She had given the order to have them brought forth with their hands tied behind their backs, and they were now standing before her. Then all of a sudden the king, who had not been expected so soon, rode into the yard. He had come on a post horse. Astonished, he demanded to know the meaning of this horrid spectacle. No one dared to tell him.

Then the ogress, in a fury at what had occurred, threw herself head first into the vat and was instantly devoured by the hideous creatures she had put there. The king could not help being sorry. She was his mother. But with a beautiful wife and two children he got over it quickly.

Little Red Ridinghood

Once upon a time there was a little village girl as pretty as could be. Her mother worshipped her. But her grandmother worshipped her even more, and the good woman had a little red hood made for her that was so becoming that everywhere she went she was called Little Red Ridinghood.

One day while warming up the oven to bake bread, her mother made some flatcakes and said, "Go see how your grandmother is. I understand she's been sick. Take her a flatcake and this little crock of butter."

Little Red Ridinghood set out at once for her grandmother's house, which was in another village. And as she went through the woods she met the old wolf, who had a good mind to eat her. He didn't dare do it, though, on account of some woodcutters who were there in the forest.

He asked her where she was going, and the poor child, not knowing it was dangerous to stop and talk to a wolf, said, "I'm going to see my grandmother and bring her a flatcake and a little crock of butter from my mother."

"Does she live very far?" said the wolf.

"Oh yes," said Little Red Ridinghood, "it's past the mill, way down there. Down that way. The first house in the village."

"Well!" said the wolf. "I'd like to go see her myself. I'll take this path and you take that one, and we'll see who gets there first."

The wolf began running as fast as he could along the shorter path, and the little girl went off down the longer path, taking her time, gathering nuts, chasing after butterflies, and picking bunches of little flowers that she found.

It wasn't long before the wolf got to grandmother's house. He knocked, *toc*, *toc*.

"Who's there?"

"It's your little girl, Little Red Ridinghood," said the wolf, disguising his voice. "I've brought you a flatcake and a little crock of butter from my mother."

The good grandmother was in bed because she felt a little ill, and she called out, "Pull the bob, the bolt'll drop!"

The wolf pulled the bob, and the door opened. He pounced on the good woman and gobbled her up in no time, because he hadn't eaten in more than three days. Then he closed the door and went and lay down in the grandmother's bed to wait for Little Red Ridinghood. After a while she came and knocked on the door, *toc*, *toc*.

"Who's there?"

At first Little Red Ridinghood was afraid, hearing the wolf's gruff voice. But thinking her grandmother had a cold, she answered, "It's your little girl, Little Red Ridinghood. I've brought you a flatcake and a little crock of butter from my mother."

Sweetening his voice a little, the wolf called out, "Pull the bob, the bolt'll drop!"

Little Red Ridinghood pulled the bob, and the door opened.

Hiding in the bed under the covers, the wolf saw her come in and said, "Put the flatcake and the little crock of butter on the hutch and come get in bed with me."

Little Red Ridinghood took off her clothes and got into bed. And when she got there, she was amazed to see what her grandmother was like undressed.

"Grandmother," she said, "what big arms you have!"

"The better to hug you, my dear."

"Grandmother, what big legs you have!"

"The better to run with, my child."

"Grandmother, what big ears you have!"

"The better to hear, my child."

"Grandmother, what big eyes you have!"

"The better to see, my child."

"Grandmother, what big teeth you have!"

"They're to eat you with!" And at these words the wicked wolf pounced on Little Red Ridinghood and ate her up.

Bluebeard

Once upon a time there was a man who had fine houses in town and in the country, with gold and silver dishes, embroidered upholstery, and carriages all covered in gold. But unfortunately this man had a blue beard, and it made him so ugly and so terrifying that there wasn't a girl or a woman who didn't run from him.

Now one of his neighbors, a lady of quality, had two flaw-lessly beautiful daughters, and he asked for one of them in marriage, leaving it to her to choose which one she would give him. But neither of these two would have him at all, and the one would foist him off on the other, unwilling to accept a man whose beard was blue. What put them off even more was that he had already been married several times and no one knew what had become of his wives.

So as to get better acquainted, Bluebeard invited both the mother and the daughters to one of his country estates along with three or four of their best friends and a few young men from the neighborhood. They stayed a week in all, and it was nothing but outings, hunts, fishing parties, dances, banquets, and suppers. Nobody slept at all, and they spent the whole night rollicking around. In short, everything turned out so well that the younger girl began to think that the host's beard was not so blue after all and that he was really quite decent. The wedding took place as soon as they got back to town.

After a month Bluebeard told his wife that he had to make a trip to the provinces of at least six weeks' duration on a matter of great importance and he wanted her to enjoy herself thoroughly while he was gone and invite her friends in. If she wished, she should take them to the country and have a good time.

"Here are the keys for the two large storerooms," he said. "And these are the ones for the gold and silver dishes that aren't used every day. And here are the ones for my strongboxes, where my gold and silver is, and the ones for the caskets where

my jewels are. And here is the master key for all the bedrooms. Now, this little key—this is the key to the closet at the end of the long gallery in the master suite. Open everything and go everywhere, but I forbid you to enter that little closet. And my forbidding you is such that if you do open it there is nothing you needn't expect from my rage."

She promised to strictly obey all the instructions she'd been given. And he, after embracing her, got into his carriage and went on his trip.

Friends and neighbor women did not wait to be invited before coming to visit the young bride, so impatient were they to see all the expensive things in her house. They hadn't dared to come while the husband was there, on account of his blue beard. It was too terrifying. And so there they were, all at once, touring the bedrooms, the closets, and the dressing rooms, each one more beautiful and more opulent than the last.

Then they went up to the storerooms, where they couldn't marvel enough at all the beautiful tapestries, beds, sofas, cabinets, pedestals, and tables—and full-length mirrors with the most beautiful, most magnificent frames anyone had ever seen, some of glass, others of silver and silver gilt.

They raved endlessly, envying their friend's good fortune, while she, meanwhile, was getting no pleasure whatever from the sight of all these riches in her impatience to go open up the closet in the master suite.

She was so driven by curiosity that without thinking how impolite it was to leave her guests she went down to the closet by a small hidden staircase—and in such haste that she almost broke her neck two or three times. When she reached the closet door, she paused for a while, thinking about her husband's warning and wondering if some harm might come to her if she disobeyed him. But the temptation was too strong for her to resist. Trembling, she took the little key and opened the door to the closet.

At first she saw nothing, because the windows were shuttered. But after a few moments she began to see that the floor was all covered with clotted blood, and in this blood were reflected the bodies of several dead women hanging up along the walls. (These were all the women that Bluebeard had married and then slaughtered one after another.) She nearly died of fright, and the key to the closet, which she had just pulled out of the lock, dropped from her hand.

When she had somewhat regained her senses, she picked up the key, closed the door, and went up to her room to compose herself a little. But she couldn't calm down, she was so shocked. Having noticed that the key to the closet was stained with blood, she wiped it two or three times, but the blood would not go away. She washed it without effect and even rubbed it with scouring powder and gritstone. The blood still remained, because the key was magic, and there was no way to

clean it completely. When the blood was removed from one side, it came back on the other.

That very same evening Bluebeard returned from his trip. He said he had received some letters along the way telling him that the business he had gone to attend to had just been settled in his favor. His wife did her best to make it look as though she were delighted to have him back so soon. The next day he asked for the keys, and she gave them to him, but with such a shaky hand that he guessed what had happened.

"Why isn't the closet key with the others?" he said.

"I must have left it upstairs on my table."

"I want it soon," said Bluebeard.

And at last, after putting him off a few times, she was forced to bring him the key. Bluebeard looked at it carefully, then he said to his wife, "Why is there blood on this key?"

"I know nothing about it," answered the poor wife, paler than death.

"If you don't know, then I do," said Bluebeard. "You wanted to get into that closet! Well, madame, you *will* get into it, and you will take your place beside the ladies you saw there."

She threw herself at her husband's feet, weeping and begging his forgiveness with all the signs of true repentance for having disobeyed him. She would have melted a stone, so beautiful she was and in such distress. But Bluebeard's heart was harder than any stone.

"You must die, madame," he said, "and right away."

"If I must die," she replied, looking at him with eyes bathed in tears, "give me a little time to say my prayers."

"I give you half of fifteen minutes and not a moment more," said Bluebeard.

As soon as she was alone she called to her sister and said, "Sister Anne (for that was her name), climb up to the tower, I beg you, and see if my brothers are coming. They promised to come visit me today, and if you see them, signal them to hurry." Sister Anne climbed to the top of the tower, and the poor thing kept crying out to her, "Anne, sister Anne, don't you see anything coming?" And sister Anne replied:

> Naught but sun's beams
> And grass that greens

Meanwhile, Bluebeard, holding a huge cutlass in his hand, was shouting to his wife with all his might, "Be down here at once, or I'll come up!"

"One more minute, please," cried his wife. And immediately she called out in a whisper, "Anne, sister Anne, don't you see anything coming?" And sister Anne replied:

> Naught but sun's beams
> And grass that greens

"Be down here at once," shouted Bluebeard, "or I'll come up!"

"I'm coming," answered his wife, and she cried out, "Anne, sister Anne, don't you see anything coming?"

"I see a great cloud of dust," replied sister Anne, "and it's coming this way."

"Is it my brothers?"

"Alas! No, my sister, it's a flock of sheep."

"Do you refuse to come down?" shouted Bluebeard.

"One more minute," replied his wife, and she cried out, "Anne, sister Anne, don't you see anything coming?"

"I see two cavaliers coming in this direction but still quite far away." A moment later she cried, "Praise God! They're my brothers! I'm signaling to them as best I can to make them hurry."

Bluebeard began to shout so mightily that the whole house shook. The poor wife went downstairs and threw herself at his feet, all in tears, and all disheveled. "That will do you no good," said Bluebeard. "You must die." Then seizing her by the hair with one hand and raising the cutlass with the other, he was just about to chop off her head. His poor wife turned toward him, and gazing at him with dying eyes begged him to give her one

brief moment to gather herself together.

"No, no!" he said. "Commend your soul to Heaven." And raising his arm—

But just at that moment there was such a heavy pounding at the door that Bluebeard stopped short.

The door was opened, and at once two cavaliers rushed in. Drawing their swords, they ran straight for Bluebeard. He recognized them as his wife's brothers, one a dragoon, the other a musketeer, and he fled instantly in an effort to escape.

But the two brothers were so close behind that they captured him before he could reach the stairs. Then they ran him through with their swords and left him to die. The poor wife was nearly as dead as her husband, and she didn't even have the strength to get up and embrace her brothers.

It turned out that Bluebeard had no heirs, and his wife therefore remained mistress of all his wealth. She used part of it to arrange a marriage between her sister Anne and a young nobleman with whom she had been in love for a long time, part of it to buy captain's rank for her two brothers, and the rest to arrange her own marriage to a very decent man who made her forget the bad time she had had with Bluebeard.

Puss in Boots

Amiller left his three children all that he had—his mill, his donkey, and his cat—and they divided it up right away without calling either the notary or the procurator, who would have promptly devoured the whole meager inheritance. The eldest got the mill, the second eldest got the donkey, and the youngest got the cat.

This youngest son could take no comfort from such a pitiful share. "My brothers can go in together and make a decent living," he said. "But what about me? When I've eaten my cat and had a muff made from its fur, I'll have to starve."

Though pretending not to, the cat overheard this and said with a grave and solemn air, "Don't be distressed, master. All you need do is get me a sack and have me a pair of boots made so I can get through the brush, and you'll see that you haven't been given so poor a share as you think."

Although the cat's master did not place much store in this, he had seen enough of his clever tricks, catching rats and mice by hanging from his hind legs or covering himself with flour and playing dead, that he did not despair of being saved from his misery.

When the cat had gotten what he asked for, he put the boots on smartly, and throwing the sack over his shoulder, he gripped the drawstring with his front paws and set off for a rabbit patch where there were a great many rabbits. He put some bran and some sow thistle into the sack. Then, stretching out as though he were dead, he waited for some young rabbit still unschooled in the wiles of this world to come rummaging in the sack for the food he had put there.

No sooner had he laid himself down than he got what he wanted. A careless young rabbit came into the sack, and the clever cat quickly pulled the drawstring and caught and killed it without a moment's thought.

Congratulating himself on his catch, he went to the royal palace and asked to speak to the king. They showed him upstairs to his majesty's apartments, and as he came before the king he made a deep bow and said, "Sire, here is a wild rabbit that I've been ordered to present to you on behalf of the lord Marquis of Carabas" (for this was the name he had decided to give his master).

"Tell your master," replied the king, "that I thank him and that he has pleased me."

Another time he went and hid in a wheat field, all the while holding his sack open. And when a couple of partridges got into it, he pulled the string and caught them both. Then he went and presented them to the king, just as he had done with the wild rabbit. The king received the two partridges, again with pleasure, and gave him a tip.

The cat went on like this for two or three months, from time to time bringing the king game from his master's coverts.

One day when he knew that the king was to go riding along the river with his daughter—who was the most beautiful princess in the world—he said to his master, "Follow my advice and your fortune is made. Simply go swimming in the river at the place I will show you, and leave the rest to me."

The Marquis of Carabas did what his cat advised, though he did not know what good would come of it. While he was swimming, the king came by and the cat began to shout with all his might, "Help! Help! The lord Marquis of Carabas is drowning!" Hearing this, the king stuck his head out the window of the coach, and recognizing the cat who had brought him game so many times, he commanded his guards to go quickly to the rescue of the lord Marquis of Carabas.

As the poor marquis was being pulled out of the river, the cat went over to the coach and told the king that while his master was swimming, thieves had come along and carried off his clothes, though of course he had cried thief with all his might. (But in fact he had craftily hidden the clothes under a huge rock.)

Immediately the king ordered his wardrobe keepers to go get one of his finest outfits for the lord Marquis of Carabas. The king showed him every courtesy, and inasmuch as the fine clothes he'd just been given showed off his good looks (for he was handsome and well built), the king's daughter found him very much to her liking. And no sooner had the Marquis of Carabas cast two or three respectful and mildly affectionate glances in her direction than she fell passionately in love.

The king insisted that he get into the coach and go for a ride.

The cat went on ahead, delighted to see that his plan was working. Meeting some peasants who were mowing a field, he said, "You good people mowing there! If you don't tell the king that the field you're mowing belongs to the lord Marquis of Carabas, you'll be chopped as fine as mincemeat!"

The king did not fail to ask the mowers whose field it was they were mowing. "This belongs to the lord Marquis of Carabas," they said, all joining in, for the cat's threat had frightened them.

"You have a nice piece of property here," said the king to the Marquis of Carabas.

"Indeed, sire," replied the marquis, "this is a field that never fails to bring a good harvest, year after year."

The clever cat, still running ahead, met some reapers, and he said, "You good people reaping there! If you don't say that all this wheat belongs to the lord Marquis of Carabas you'll be chopped as fine as mincemeat!"

A moment later the king passed by and wanted to know who owned all the wheat that he saw. "This belongs to the lord Marquis of Carabas," answered the reapers. And again the king admired it together with the marquis. Running ahead of the coach, the cat kept saying the same thing to everybody he met, and the king was amazed at the great wealth of the lord Marquis of Carabas.

The clever cat came at last to a beautiful castle, the master of which was an ogre, the richest that had ever been known, for all the lands the king had passed through belonged to this castle. After taking care to find out who this ogre was and what he could do, the cat asked to speak with him, saying that he did not want to pass so close to the castle without having the honor of paying his respects. The ogre received him as civilly as an ogre can and invited him to sit down.

"They tell me," said the cat, "that you have the power to change yourself into all sorts of animals and that you can become a lion or an elephant, for example."

"That is true," replied the ogre gruffly. "I will show you. Now watch me become a lion."

The cat was so frightened to see a lion right in front of him that he headed straight for the roof—and not without hardship and danger, on account of his boots, which were no good for walking on tiles. After a while, seeing that the ogre had abandoned this guise, the cat came back down and confessed that he had been badly frightened.

"I've been told furthermore," said the cat, "though I don't know if I can believe it, that you also have the power to change

into the smallest of animals, to become a rat, for example, or a mouse. I must say I find this quite impossible."

"Impossible?" said the ogre. "You shall see." And that very moment he changed himself into a mouse and began to run along the floor. No sooner had the cat caught sight of it than he pounced on it and ate it up.

Meanwhile the king, passing by, saw the ogre's fine castle and decided to go inside. Hearing the rumble of the coach as it came over the drawbridge, the cat ran to meet it and said to the king, "Your majesty, welcome to the castle of the lord Marquis of Carabas."

"Why, Marquis!" cried the king. "This castle is yours, too? There could be nothing finer than this courtyard and all these buildings around it. With your permission let us see the inside."

The marquis gave his hand to the young princess, and following the king, who went in first, they entered a great hall. There they found a magnificent supper the ogre had prepared for his friends, who were coming to see him that very day. But they hadn't dared to come in when they heard the king was there.

The king, charmed by the excellent qualities of the lord Marquis of Carabas—as much so as his daughter, who was thoroughly enamored—and seeing the great wealth that he possessed, said to him, after drinking five or six draughts, "It depends only on you, marquis, as to whether you shall be my son-in-law." The marquis, making a deep bow, accepted the honor the king had conferred upon him, and that very day he married the princess.

As for the cat, he became a great lord and never ran after mice again, except for his own amusement.

Diamonds and Toads

Once upon a time there was a widow who had two daughters, one of whom—the older girl—looked and acted so much like the widow herself that whoever saw the one saw the other. The two of them were so unpleasant and so vain that no one could stand to be with them. But the younger one, in her gentleness and kind ways, was the true image of her father. In addition she was one of the most beautiful girls ever seen.

Since people are naturally attracted to others who are like themselves, this mother doted on the older daughter. At the same time she hated the younger girl and made her eat in the kitchen and work all the time.

On top of everything else the poor child had to go draw water twice a day at a good half-league's distance from the house and carry back a huge pitcherful. One day while she was at the spring a poor woman came up to her and asked for a drink.

"Why yes, good mother," said the beautiful girl. And immediately rinsing the pitcher, she drew some water from the nicest part of the spring and gave it to her, holding the pitcher so that she could drink more easily. When she had finished drinking, the good woman said to her, "You are so beautiful, so good, and so kind that I cannot help but make you a wish (for she was a fairy who had changed herself into an old village woman in order to see how far this young girl's kindness would go).

"And here," continued the fairy, "is my wish. With every word you speak a flower or a jewel shall come out of your mouth."

When the beautiful girl got back to the house, her mother

scolded her for staying so long at the spring. "I'm sorry to have been so long, mother," said the poor girl. And as she spoke these words two roses, two pearls, and two large diamonds came out of her mouth.

"What am I seeing?" cried the mother, astounded. "Why, I thought I saw pearls and diamonds coming out of her mouth! What's the meaning of this, dear daughter?" (It was the first time she had ever addressed her as "daughter.") The poor child innocently told her what had happened, and not without spewing an infinite number of diamonds.

"Really!" said the mother. "I must send my daughter down there at once. Look, Fanny! See what's coming out of your sister's mouth when she talks. Don't you wish it were you? All you have to do is go down to the spring and draw water, and when a poor woman asks you for a drink you give it to her very politely."

"That would be a pretty sight!" said the ill-mannered sister. "Me, going to the spring!"

"I insist that you go," said the mother, "and right this minute."

She went, but grumbling all the way, taking the finest silver flask in the house. No sooner had she arrived at the spring than a magnificently dressed lady came out of the woods and asked for a drink. It was the same fairy who had appeared to her sister, but looking and acting like a princess in order to see just how far this girl's rudeness would go.

"Is that what I came for? To give you a drink?" said the haughty, ill-mannered girl. "I suppose I brought this silver flask just for my lady's drinking! I like *that*. But here, drink if you want."

"You are not very kind," said the fairy, without getting angry. "Well, since you are so inconsiderate, I must make this wish. With every word you speak a snake or a toad shall come out of your mouth."

When her mother caught sight of her she cried, "Well, daughter!"

"Well, mother!" answered the ill-mannered girl, spewing two vipers and two toads.

"Heavens!" cried the Mother. "What am I seeing? Her sister is responsible for this. And she shall pay for it." Then she ran at once to give her a beating.

The poor child fled away and hid in the woods nearby. The king's son, just coming back from hunting, found her there and seeing how beautiful she was asked her why she was all alone and crying.

"Oh, sir, it's my mother. She chased me out of the house."

Seeing five or six pearls drop from her mouth, and as many diamonds, the prince asked her how this could be, and she told him the whole story. He fell in love with her, and realizing that the gift she had was worth more than anything that could possibly be presented to him if he married someone else, he carried her off to the palace of the king, who was his father, and there he married her.

As for the sister, she made herself so hateful that her own mother chased her away. The poor thing wandered about without finding anyone who was willing to take her in, until at last she curled up in a corner of the woods and died.

Cinderella

Once upon a time there was a nobleman who took as his second wife the proudest and haughtiest woman anyone had ever seen. This woman had two daughters who were exactly like herself in every way. The husband, by his first wife, had one daughter, whose gentleness and goodness were unsurpassed. But this she had gotten from her mother, who had been the most admirable person in the world.

No sooner was the wedding over than the stepmother showed how mean she could be. She couldn't stand the excellent qualities of that young child, who made her own daughters seem all the more hateful. And so she gave her the worst chores in the house.

It was she who had to wash the dishes and scrub the stairs and clean the mistress's bedroom and the bedrooms of the young mistresses who were the stepmother's daughters. She slept in a garret at the very top of the house on a miserable mattress, while her sisters had rooms with parquet floors and beds in the very latest style and full-length mirrors.

The poor girl endured everything patiently. She didn't dare complain to her father because his wife ruled him completely and he would only have scolded her. When she had finished her chores she would go and sit among the cinders in the chimney corner, and for this reason she was known around the house as Cinderbottom. The younger daughter, who was not quite so coarse as her older sister, called her Cinderella. Yet Cinderella, with her miserable clothes, was nevertheless a hundred times more beautiful than her sisters, no matter how magnificently they might be dressed.

Now it came about that the king's son gave a ball, to which everyone of importance was asked to come. And our two young ladies were among those invited, because they cut quite a figure in the fashionable circles in that country. And so there they were, all aglow and all aflutter, choosing the outfits and the hairstyles that would be the most becoming to them—all of which meant more work for Cinderella, for it was she who ironed her sisters' linen collars and pleated their ruffles.

They talked of nothing but what they would wear. "I," said the older girl, "shall wear my red velvet with the English lace."

"Well," said the younger one, "I'm going to have a plain petticoat. But then I'll wear my overdress with the gold flowers and my diamond brooch. And there's nothing plain about that!"

They sent to the hairdresser to have double rows of horn-curls made up, and they ordered face patches from the patch-maker. Then they called in Cinderella to ask her opinion, because it was she who had good taste.

Cinderella gave them the best advice in the world and even offered to dress their hair, which they very much wanted her to do.

"Cinderella," they asked, as she was fixing their hair,

"wouldn't you like to be going to the ball?"

"Oh, ladies! You're making fun of me. It wouldn't be proper for me to go."

"You're right. People would laugh if they saw a cinderbottom heading for the ball." And anyone but Cinderella, hearing this, would have left their hair in a tangle. But she was so good-natured she coiffed them to perfection.

For nearly two days they went without eating, they were so excited. More than a dozen laces were broken, pulling in their stays to make their waists thinner, and they were constantly in front of the mirror.

At last the happy day arrived. Off they went, and Cinderella followed them with her eyes as long as possible. When she could no longer see them she began to cry.

Finding her all in tears, her godmother asked her what was the matter. "I wish . . . I wish"—she was crying so hard she couldn't finish. But her godmother, who was a fairy, said, "You wish you could go to the ball. Isn't that it?"

"Oh yes," said Cinderella, sighing.

"Well," said her godmother, "will you be a good girl? I'll arrange it so that you can go." Then she took her to her room and said, "Run into the garden and bring me a pumpkin."

Cinderella went at once and got the nicest one she could find and brought it to her godmother, though she couldn't imagine how a pumpkin might get her to the ball. Her godmother hollowed it out, leaving only the rind. Then she tapped it with

her wand, and the pumpkin turned into a beautiful coach all covered in gold.

Next she looked in her mousetrap and found six mice, all alive. She asked Cinderella to lift the door to the cage a little, and as the mice came out, one by one, she tapped them with her wand. Each mouse was immediately changed into a beautiful horse, giving her a team of six horses in all, dappled a beautiful mouse gray.

She didn't know what to do for a coachman. Then Cinderella said, "Let me see if there isn't a rat in the rattrap. We could make a coachman out of that."

"You're right," said the godmother. "Go see." Cinderella brought her the rattrap, and in it were three huge rats. The fairy picked one of the three—on account of its superior whiskers—and as she touched it with her wand it was changed into a stout coachman with one of the finest moustaches ever seen.

Then she said, "Go to the garden. There you'll find six lizards behind the watering can. Bring them to me."

And no sooner had she brought them than the godmother turned them into six liveried footmen. They climbed right up on the back of the coach and stood there holding fast as though they had never done anything else in their lives.

Then the fairy said to Cinderella, "Well, here's what you'll need to go to the ball. Don't you like it?"

"Yes, but am I to go in these ugly clothes?"

Her godmother simply touched her with her wand and in that moment her dress was changed into a dress of gold-and-silver cloth all covered with precious stones. Then she gave her a pair of glass slippers, the prettiest in the world.

All dressed up, she climbed into the coach. But her godmother told her that above all things she must not stay past midnight, warning her that if she stayed at the ball a moment later her coach would become a pumpkin again, her horses mice, and her footmen lizards. And even her old clothes would reappear.

She promised her godmother that she would leave the ball before midnight, without fail. Then off she went, beside herself with joy.

When the king's son was told that a great princess had arrived, whom nobody knew, he rushed to meet her. He gave her his hand as she got out of the coach and led her into the hall where the guests were. There was a great silence then. The dancing stopped, the violins no longer played, so intently did everyone turn his attention upon the great charms of this unknown person. The only sound was a confused murmur of "Ah, how beautiful she is!"

The king himself, old as he was, could not help but gaze at her and whisper to the queen that it had been a long time since he had seen anyone so beautiful and so charming. All the ladies were intent upon studying her hair and her clothes, so as to have the same thing themselves the very next day, assuming that fine enough fabrics could be found and dressmakers with sufficient skill.

The king's son put her in the place of honor and then invited her to dance. She danced with such grace that people admired her all the more. A beautiful supper was served, but the young prince was so taken up with gazing at Cinderella that he could eat nothing at all.

She went and sat next to her sisters and showered them with kindness, sharing the oranges and lemons the prince had given her. At this they were amazed, because they didn't know her at all.

While they were chatting, Cinderella heard the clock strike a quarter to twelve. She immediately made a deep curtsy to the assembled guests and left as quickly as she could.

When she got home she went and found her godmother, and

after thanking her told her that she wished she could go to the ball again the next day, for the king's son had invited her. While she was telling her godmother everything that had happened at the ball, the two sisters knocked at the door. Cinderella went to let them in.

"How long you were!" she said, yawning and rubbing her eyes, and stretching as if she had just woken up. Yet in fact she had had no thought of sleeping since they had last seen each other.

"If you had come to the ball," said one of her sisters, "you wouldn't have gotten so tired. The most beautiful princess came that anybody would ever hope to see, and she showered us with kindness. She gave us oranges and lemons!"

Cinderella was beside herself with joy and asked them the name of this princess. But they told her that no one knew, and that the king's son was very upset about it and would give anything in the world to know who she was.

Cinderella smiled and said, "Was she really that beautiful? Heavens, you're lucky! Couldn't I see her? Oh, Miss Javotte, let me borrow your yellow dress, the everyday one."

"Really!" said Javotte. "Wouldn't *that* be nice. Lend my dress to a repulsive cinderbottom! I'd have to be mad."

Cinderella fully expected this refusal and was just as glad to hear it, because she wouldn't have known what to do if her sister had actually lent her the dress.

The next day the two sisters went off to the ball and so did Cinderella, dressed even more elegantly than the first time. The king's son was constantly at her side and kept flattering her with soft words. The young lady found it by no means tiresome. Forgetting her godmother's warning, she heard the first stroke of midnight while still thinking it wasn't quite eleven. She arose and fled away as lightly as a doe. The prince chased after her, unable to catch her. She dropped one of her glass slippers, however, and the prince, very carefully, picked it up.

Cinderella reached home all out of breath, without her coach, without her footmen, and in her miserable clothes. Nothing was left of all her magnificence except one of her little slippers, the mate to the one she had dropped.

The guards at the palace gate were asked if they had seen a princess go by. Only a girl in rags, they said, and more like a peasant than a lady.

When her two sisters returned from the ball, Cinderella asked them if they had had a good time again and if the beautiful lady had been there.

They said yes. But she had fled away at the stroke of midnight, they said, and so hurriedly that she had dropped one of her little glass slippers, the prettiest thing in the world. And the

king's son had picked it up and had done nothing but gaze at it for the rest of the ball. And no doubt he was very much in love with the beautiful owner of the little slipper.

What they said was true. Indeed, a few days later the king's son had it proclaimed to the sound of trumpets that he would marry the girl whose foot exactly fit the slipper. It was tried first on princesses, then on duchesses, and then on all the court, but without success.

When it was brought to the house where the two sisters

lived, each in turn did everything she could to make her foot go into the slipper. But it was no use.

Cinderella was watching them, and recognizing her slipper she said laughingly, "I wonder if it wouldn't fit me."

Her sisters burst out laughing and mocked her. But the nobleman who was conducting the test, having looked closely at Cinderella and finding her quite beautiful, said that this would be proper and that he had been commanded to try it on every young woman. He had Cinderella sit down. Then lifting the slipper to her little foot he saw that it went in without difficulty. It fit her as if poured on like wax.

The astonishment of the two sisters, great as it was, was even greater when Cinderella drew the other little slipper out of her pocket and put it on. Just then the godmother appeared and, touching her wand to Cinderella's dress, made it more magnificent than ever.

Her two sisters recognized her as the beautiful lady they had seen at the ball. They threw themselves at her feet, begging her to forgive them for all the harsh treatment they had caused her to suffer. Cinderella raised them up and embraced them, telling them she pardoned them with all her heart and hoped they would always love her.

She was taken to the prince in her magnificent clothes, and he found her even more beautiful than before. A few days later they were married.

Cinderella was as good as she was beautiful. She had her two sisters come stay at the palace and arranged for them to be married that same day to two great lords of the court.

Rickety Topknot

Once upon a time there was a queen who gave birth to a son so ugly and so misshapen that for a long time people doubted that he was human. A fairy who was present at his birth gave assurance, however, that he would not fail to be well liked because he would be possessed with great intelligence. She even said that on account of a wish she had just made for him he would be able to give the woman he loved most the same intellect he himself would have. All this made the poor queen feel a little better, for she was painfully distressed at having brought such a horrid-looking creature into the world.

True enough, no sooner had the child begun to speak than he said all sorts of witty things. And no matter what he did there was something so indescribably clever about it that people were charmed. I neglected to mention that he came into the world with a little tuft of hair on his head, and for this reason he was called Rickety Topknot, Rickety being his family name.

Now it happened that seven or eight years later the queen of a neighboring kingdom gave birth to twin daughters. The first to be born was as fair as day itself, and the queen was so delighted that it was feared her great excitement might do her some harm.

The same fairy was there who had attended the birth of little Rickety Topknot, and to temper the queen's joy she declared that the little princess would have no wit at all and would be just as stupid as she was beautiful.

At this the queen was deeply mortified. But a few moments later she suffered an even greater shock, for the second daughter to be born was extremely ugly.

"Madame, don't be so upset," said the fairy. "She'll make up for it in other ways. She'll be so clever that people will hardly notice she isn't beautiful."

"May heaven grant it!" replied the queen. "But isn't there any way for the older girl who is so beautiful to have just a bit of cleverness?"

"Madame, I can do nothing for her in the way of cleverness," said the fairy. "But when it comes to beauty I can do everything. And since there is nothing I wouldn't do to make you happy, I am going to give her the power to make the one person who pleases her beautiful, or handsome."

As the two princesses grew, their good qualities grew with them, and people everywhere talked of nothing but the older girl's beauty and the younger girl's wit. But their faults, too, increased with age, and the younger girl grew uglier before one's very eyes, while the older girl became more stupid day by day. Either she didn't answer when someone spoke to her or she said something foolish. At the same time she was so clumsy she couldn't set four pieces of china on the mantel without breaking one of them, or drink a glass of water without spilling half of it on her clothes.

Though beauty is a great advantage for any young woman, nevertheless whenever there was company the younger girl nearly always won out over her sister. At first everybody would head for the prettier one to get a good look at her and

admire her, but soon thereafter they would go over to the cleverer one to hear all the delightful things she had to say.

Amazingly, in less than a quarter of an hour the older girl would have no one left at her side and everybody would be clustered around her younger sister.

Stupid as she was, the older girl took note of this and would have gladly given all her beauty for half her sister's wit. The queen, although she was a wise woman, could not help but scold her for her stupidity, and more than once. And at this the poor princess nearly died of shame.

One day while off in the woods by herself, lamenting her misfortune, she saw a little man coming toward her. He was quite ugly and quite unappealing, yet dressed most magnificently. It was young prince Rickety Topknot who, having fallen in love with her portrait, which was circulated everywhere, had left his father's kingdom in order to have the pleasure of actually seeing her and speaking with her.

Thrilled at finding her all alone like this, he approached her with the greatest imaginable reverence and courtesy. He paid his respects to her in the usual manner. Then, having noticed how gloomy she was, he said, "Dear lady, I don't understand how someone as beautiful as you are can be so sad, for although I pride myself on having seen countless beautiful young women I can't say I have ever seen anyone whose beauty comes close to yours."

"It pleases you to say so, sir," replied the princess, and she stopped at that.

"Beauty is such a great advantage," continued Rickety Topknot, "that it takes the place of everything else. And if you have it, I don't see that anything could really bother you."

"I'd rather be as ugly as you are and be intelligent than be as beautiful and as stupid as I am," said the princess.

"Dear lady, if you think you do not have intellect, that's the best proof in the world that you do in fact have it. That's the way it is. The more of it you have, the less you *think* you have."

"I don't know about that," said the princess. "But I know well enough that I am very stupid, and it's that that hurts me so."

"If that's all that's troubling you, dear lady, I can easily put an end to it."

"How?" said the princess.

"I have the power to give infinite cleverness to the woman I love best," said Rickety Topknot, "and you, dear lady, are that woman. It's entirely up to you to be as clever as anyone could possibly be, provided you are willing to be my wife."

The princess was astounded and said not a word.

"I can see that this idea disturbs you," said Rickety Topknot, "and I am not surprised. But I give you a full year to make up your mind."

The princess had so little wit and at the same time so great a

desire to have some that she fancied a year would never end, and so she said yes to his proposal.

No sooner had she promised Rickety Topknot that she would marry him in a year to the day, than she suddenly felt herself a different person. She found within her an unbelievable ability to say whatever she liked and to say it gracefully, with ease and naturalness. She immediately struck up an elegant and prolonged conversation with Rickety Topknot in which she shone so brilliantly that he wondered if he hadn't given her more wit than he had kept for himself.

When she got back to the palace the courtiers couldn't get over this sudden and extraordinary change, for as senseless as everything was that they'd heard her say before, what they were hearing now was filled with meaning and wonderfully clever. The whole court was overjoyed.

The only one who was less than happy was the younger daughter. Now that she no longer had the advantage of being more clever she seemed nothing but a frightful hag alongside her sister.

The king himself now followed her advice, and sometimes he even held his council of state in her chamber.

News of this change spread rapidly, and all the young princes from nearby kingdoms outdid themselves trying to win her favor. Nearly all of them asked for her hand in marriage. But none had enough wit to suit her, and she heard what they all had to say without promising herself to any of them.

Of those who came there was one so powerful, however, and so rich, so clever, and so handsome that she couldn't help but feel kindly disposed toward him. Her father took note of this and told her she could make her own choice of a husband. She need only speak her mind.

But the more intelligence one has the harder it is to make a decision in a case like this. And so, after thanking her father, she asked him to give her some time to consider.

In order to concentrate more easily on what she should do she chanced to go for a stroll in the same wood where she had met Rickety Topknot. As she was walking along, deep in thought, she heard a rumbling noise under her path, as though a great many people were bustling to and fro.

Listening more closely, she heard someone say, "Bring me that pan." Another said, "Hand me that boiler." And another, "Put some wood on that fire."

Just then the earth opened up and beneath her she saw what seemed to be a huge kitchen full of cooks, scullions, and every sort of functionary needed to put on a sumptuous banquet. Then out came an army of twenty or thirty chefs. They went and settled themselves around a long table in an open space beneath the trees. With larding pins in hand and with the fox-tails attached to their caps tucked up around their ears, they set to work in rhythm to the sound of a melodious chant.

Amazed at such a spectacle, the princess asked them who they were doing this for.

"This," answered the one who was first in command, "is for Prince Rickety Topknot, whose wedding will take place tomorrow."

Even more surprised than at first and suddenly remembering that a year before to the day she had promised to marry Prince Rickety Topknot, the princess felt as though the ground had been swept from beneath her. The reason she hadn't remem-

bered is that when she had made this promise she had been a fool, and in accepting the new cleverness the prince had given her she had forgotten all her old stupidities.

She had not gone another thirty paces when Rickety Topknot himself appeared before her, all dressed up like a prince on his way to be married.

"As you can see, dear lady," he said, "I have kept my promise, and I have no doubt that you have come to keep yours, to give me your hand, and to make me the happiest of all men."

"I frankly confess," replied the princess, "that I still haven't made my decision, and that I don't believe I will ever be able to make the decision you are hoping for."

"You astound me, dear lady," said Rickety Topknot.

"I can well believe it," said the princess, "and certainly, if I were dealing with a crude and witless man, I would be most embarrassed. 'A princess is only as good as her word,' he would tell me. And, 'You have to marry me because you promised.' But the one with whom I speak is a man of the world and of the utmost intelligence. Therefore I am certain he will listen to reason. As you know, when I was but a fool, even then I could not be sure about marrying you. How can you think, with the wit you have given me, which makes me even more particular about people than I used to be, that I can now be sure of what I wasn't sure of then? If you really thought you were going to marry me, you made a great mistake when you took away my stupidity, enabling me to see more clearly than I ever did before."

"If a man of no wit," replied Rickety Topknot, "can be allowed, as you have just said, to accuse you of not keeping your promise, how, dear lady, can you expect me not to do the same, when it is a question of my whole life's happiness? Does it make sense for people who have intelligence to be worse off than people who have none? Can you who have so much and who wanted it so badly pretend that this is so? But please, let's come to the point. Aside from my ugliness, is there anything about me that displeases you? Are you dissatisfied with my birth, my wit, my character, my manners?"

"Not at all," replied the princess. "I like everything about you that you have mentioned."

"If that's the case," said Rickety Topknot, "happiness will be mine, for it is within your power to make me the most attractive of all men."

"How can that be?" said the princess.

"It will happen of itself," replied Rickety Topknot, "if you will love me enough to wish it were so. And in case you have any doubts, dear lady, be advised that the same fairy who the day I was born gave me the power to make the woman of my choice intelligent also gave you the power to make the one who loves you handsome, should you wish to do him that favor."

"If that is so," said the princess, "then I wish with all my heart you would become the most handsome and most appealing prince in the world, and I grant you these qualities in as great a measure as I possess them myself."

No sooner had the princess pronounced these words than Rickety Topknot appeared to her as the handsomest man in the world, the most perfectly built, and the most appealing she had ever seen.

Some say that it was not the fairy's magic that was at work but that love alone had caused this transformation. They say that having turned her thoughts toward her lover's determination, his good judgment, and all his fine qualities of heart and mind, the princess no longer noticed that his body was deformed or that his face was ugly.

They say that to her the hump on his back only seemed to increase his stature, and that instead of seeing him hobble along lamely, as before, she found that he bent forward attentively in a manner most charming to see. And his eyes, which were squinty, only seemed the more brilliant—if cross-eyed, he merely seemed the more crazed with love. And finally, his great red nose, to her, seemed soldierlike and heroic.

However the case may be, the princess immediately promised to marry him, provided he obtained the consent of her father, the king. And the king, seeing that his daughter had such a high regard for Rickety Topknot, whom he knew to be a wise and clever prince, gladly accepted him as his son-in-law. The wedding was held the very next day, just as Rickety Topknot had predicted and in accordance with the arrangements he had already made a long time before.

Hop o' My Thumb

Once upon a time there lived a woodcutter and his wife who had seven children, all boys. The oldest was just ten years old and the youngest was all of seven. It's surprising that this woodcutter had so many children so close together, but his wife got right down to business and had them two or more at a time.

They were extremely poor, and their seven children were a great burden, for not one of them was old enough to earn his own living. What distressed them even more was that the young-est was as puny as could be and didn't even speak. And although this was simply because he was so good-natured, they took it to mean that he was stupid. And he was extremely small. Indeed, when he was born he was scarce-ly bigger than a thumb, and for this reason he was called Hop o' My Thumb.

This poor child was the scapegoat of the family. They blamed him for everything. Yet he was the sharpest and cleverest of all the brothers, and if he spoke little he listened much.

There came a very terrible year, and there was so much hunger and starvation that these poor people decided to get rid of their children. One night when the woodcutter was sitting by the fire with his wife, and the children were in bed, he said to her, his heart crushed with grief, "You know we can't afford to feed our children anymore, and I can't bear to see them die right before my eyes. So I've decided to take them out in the woods tomorrow and let them get lost. It'll be easy, because they'll be having a good time gathering firewood and all we'll have to do is slip away when they're not looking."

"Heavens," cried the wife, "would you have your own children get lost?" Her husband pointed out to her how poor they were, but in vain. She wouldn't agree to it. Poor she might be, but she was their mother. And yet, when she considered how painful it would be for her to see them die of hunger, she did agree to it and went to bed in tears.

Hop o' My Thumb heard everything they said. Lying in bed he could tell they were talking about something important, and he got up quietly and slipped under his father's stool so he could listen without being seen. Then he went back to bed. But he didn't sleep a wink the rest of the night, thinking about what he should do.

In the morning he got up early and went down to the edge of the stream. He filled his pockets with little white stones, then returned to the house.

Off they went, and Hop 'o My Thumb said not a word to his brothers about what he knew. They got to a very dense part of the forest where they couldn't see each other ten paces away. Then the woodcutter started to chop wood, while the children gathered branches to make kindling. Seeing them busy at their work, the mother and father gradually moved away, then all of a sudden hurried off down an obscure little path.

When the children saw that they were alone, they started shouting and crying as hard as they could. Hop o' My Thumb let them cry, for all along the way he had dropped the little white stones that he had carried in his pocket. "Brothers," he said, "don't be afraid. Mother and father have left us here, but I'll take you right back home. Just follow me." And they followed him, and he led them all the way to their house by the same path they had taken into the woods.

At first they didn't dare go inside. Instead they all leaned against the door to hear what their mother and father were saying.

Now, the moment the woodcutter and his wife had returned home the lord of the manor had sent them ten crowns that he had owed them for a long time and that they had lost all hope of ever getting. This put new life into them, for the poor souls were dying of hunger. Immediately the woodcutter sent his wife to the butcher's, and because it had been so long since she had eaten she bought three times as much meat as two people would have needed for their dinner.

When they had eaten their fill, the wife said, "Oh dear, now where are our poor children? They'd have had a nice supper with these leftovers. But oh no, John, you had to get rid of them. I told you we'd be sorry. What are they doing now in those woods? Dear God, maybe they've been eaten up by wolves. You're a monster to get rid of your children like that!"

The woodcutter finally lost his temper, for she said it twenty times and more: "You'll be sorry" and "I told you so." He threatened to beat her if she didn't shut up. It wasn't that he felt less badly than his wife. It was just that she was wearing him out, and he was one of those people who greatly admire a woman who talks sense but can't stand a woman who's always right.

The wife was in tears. "Oh dear, where are my children now? My poor children!" Finally she said it so loudly that the children at the door, overhearing her, burst out crying, "Here we are! Here we are!"

She rushed to open the door and hugged them, saying, "Oh my dear children, I'm so glad to see you again! You must be tired, and you must be hungry. Oh, Peterkin, you're all muddy! Come, let me wash your face." This Peterkin was her oldest boy, the one she loved best because he was a bit of a redhead, and she was a trifle redheaded herself.

They sat down to the table and ate with an appetite that did their parents good to see. All talking at once, they told how scary it had been in the forest.

The good souls were delighted to have their children home again, and their happiness lasted as long as the ten crowns lasted. But when the money was spent, they fell back into their old despair and decided to get rid of them again.

So as not to make the same mistake twice, they would take them farther away this time. But they couldn't talk about it quietly enough for Hop o' My Thumb not to hear, and he made up his mind to use the same trick as before.

When he got up early the next morning to go gather the pebbles, however, he found that the door to the house was double-locked, and his plan didn't work. He was wondering what to do when it suddenly occurred to him, as the woodcutter's wife handed them each a piece of bread for their breakfast, that he could use the bread, instead of pebbles, by dropping bits of it along the paths that they would take. And so he stuffed it into his pocket.

The mother and father led them into the deepest and darkest part of the forest, then they slipped away by a secret path and left them there. Hop o' My Thumb didn't worry very much, because he thought he could easily find his way on account of the bread he'd scattered everywhere they'd been. But he was quite surprised at not being able to find a single crumb. Birds had come along and eaten it all up.

Now they were in great trouble, for the more they walked

the more lost they got, going deeper and deeper into the forest. Night came, and a great wind blew up, giving them a terrible fright. They imagined they heard howling wolves coming to eat them from every direction. They hardly dared speak to each other or turn their heads. Then heavy rains fell, soaking them to the bone. At every step they tripped and fell in the mire and got up all muddy because they couldn't see where to put their hands.

Hop o' My Thumb climbed to the top of a tree to see if he could see anything. Looking all around, he saw a tiny light, like a candle, but way in the distance beyond the forest. He climbed down the tree, but when he reached the ground he could no longer see a thing, much to his dismay. Nevertheless, after he and his brothers had walked for some time in the direction in which he had seen the light, he saw it again, just as they came out of the woods.

At last they reached the house where the candle was, though not without many a scare, for again and again they lost sight of it every time they went into a hollow. They knocked, and a nice woman came to the door and asked them what they wanted.

Hop o' My Thumb explained to her that they were poor

children who had been lost in the forest. He asked her to take pity on them and give them a place to sleep. Seeing how pretty they all were, the woman started to cry and said, "Oh dear, you poor children, what have you done? Don't you know this house belongs to an ogre who eats little children?"

"Oh, madame!" replied Hop o' My Thumb, trembling all over, and his brothers too. "What shall we do? Surely the wolves in the forest will eat us tonight unless you take us in. If it has to be, we'd rather it were your husband who ate us. But maybe he will take pity on us, if you plead with him."

Thinking she could hide them from her husband until morning, the ogre's wife took them in and had them get warm in front of a tremendous fire—for there was a whole sheep on the spit for the ogre's supper.

Just as they were beginning to get warm they heard three or four loud knocks at the door. It was the ogre coming home. His wife immediately hid them under the bed and went to open the door.

The first thing the ogre wanted to know was where his supper was and whether some wine had been drawn, and right away he sat down to the table. The sheep, still all bloody, was just the way he liked it. Then he sniffed to the right and to the left and said, "I smell fresh meat."

"Oh," said his wife, "you must be smelling that calf I just dressed."

"*I tell you I smell fresh meat*," replied the ogre, eyeing his wife askance. "There's something going on here that I don't understand."

With these words he rose from the table and headed straight for the bed. "Aha," he said, "so you tried to cheat me, you wretched woman! I don't know what keeps me from eating you, too. You're lucky you're such an old beast. Well, here's a nice bag of game! And just what I'll need when I entertain those three ogre friends of mine who are coming to see me in a few days!"

One by one he pulled them out from under the bed. The poor children got on their knees and begged for mercy, but they were up against the cruelest of all ogres, who far from pitying them was already devouring them with his eyes and telling his wife what dainty morsels they'd be after she'd fixed them in a nice sauce.

He went and got a huge knife, and as he closed in on those poor children he sharpened it against a long stone that he held in his left hand. He had already taken one of them into his clutches when his wife said to him, "What are you getting into at this hour of the day? Won't you have enough time for that tomorrow?"

"Shut up," said the ogre. "They'll be more cured and tender this way."

"But look at the meat you've already got. Here's a calf, two sheep, and half a hog!"

"You're right," said the ogre. "Give them a good supper, so they won't get thin, and put them to bed."

The good woman was overjoyed and served them a nice supper indeed, but they were so frightened they couldn't eat. As for the ogre, he went back to his drinking, well pleased to be having something this good to feed his friends, and he drank a dozen more draughts than usual. As it went to his head somewhat, he had to go off to bed.

Now the ogre had seven daughters, who were just children still, and these little ogresses all had the rosiest of complexions, for they ate raw meat the same as their father did. Their eyes were small and gray, however, and completely round, and they had hooked noses and huge mouths with long sharp teeth spaced wide apart. As yet they were not terribly wicked, though they gave much promise of being so, for even now they would bite into little children and suck their blood.

They had been put to bed early, and all seven were in one enormous bed, each with a gold crown on her head. In the same room was another bed just as large, and it was here that the ogre's wife put the seven little boys. After that she went and lay down next to her husband.

Hop o' My Thumb had noticed that the ogre's daughters had

gold crowns on their heads and, fearing the ogre might have some second thoughts about slitting their throats that very evening, he got up shortly before midnight and took off his and his brothers' night caps and went and very gently put them on the heads of the ogre's seven daughters—after having removed their gold crowns, which he placed on the heads of his brothers and himself. That way the ogre would take them for his daughters and his daughters for the little boys whose throats he was supposed to slit.

Everything went as planned. The ogre woke up exactly at midnight and had second thoughts about putting off till tomorrow what he could very well do that night. All of a sudden he jumped out of bed, and reaching for his big knife, he said, "Let's see how the little rascals are doing. No need to put this off."

He felt his way up to his daughters' room and went over to the little boys' bed. All were asleep except Hop o' My Thumb, who was frightened indeed when he felt the ogre's hand groping for his head and for his brothers' heads, too.

Feeling the gold crowns, the ogre said, "Well, that would have been a pretty thing to do! I must have drunk too much wine at supper."

Then he went straight to the bed where his daughters were, and feeling the little boys' night caps he said, "Ah, so here you are, my stalwarts! Let's get to work!"

As he uttered these words, and without thinking twice, he

cut the throats of his seven daughters.

Well pleased with what he'd done, he went and lay down beside his wife again. As soon as Hop o' My Thumb heard the ogre snoring, he woke his brothers and told them to put on their clothes and follow him at once. Very quietly they slipped down into the garden and leaped over the wall. They ran almost all night, quivering the whole time and not knowing where they were going.

When the ogre woke up he said to his wife, "Go upstairs and dress those little rascals who were here last night."

The ogre's wife was astonished at her husband's kindness, never doubting what he might mean by "dressing" them. And believing he had given her orders to go put their clothes on, she went on up.

Indeed she had quite a surprise when she saw her seven daughters with their throats slit, floating in their own blood. She immediately fainted (for that's the first thing most women do in such circumstances).

Afraid that he'd given his wife too big a job, the ogre went upstairs to help her out. He was no less astounded than his wife when he laid eyes on the horrid sight.

"Ah! What have I done?" he cried. "Those little wretches will pay me for this and right away!"

Then he threw a potful of water in his wife's face, and when he had revived her he said, "Quick, give me my seven-league boots so I can catch up to them."

He set off into the countryside, and after running a good distance in every direction, he finally came the same way the poor children had gone. They were no more than a hundred steps from their father's house, but they could see the ogre going from mountain to mountain and crossing rivers as though they were tiny streamlets. Hop o' My Thumb, noticing a hollow rock nearby, hid his six brothers inside it and crawled in himself, all the while watching to see what the ogre would do.

The ogre was beginning to get very tired from his long and pointless travels (for seven-league boots are extremely tiring for the person who wears them) and he wanted to rest. Just by chance he came and settled down on the rock where the little boys were hiding. Exhausted, he fell asleep after lying there for a bit and started to snore so terrifically that the poor children were no less frightened than when he had raised his huge knife to cut their throats.

Hop o' My Thumb was not as afraid as his brothers, and he told them to run for the house as fast as they could while the ogre was sleeping so soundly and not to worry about him. They took him at his word and rushed to the house.

Then Hop o' My Thumb went up to the ogre and gently pulled off his boots and put them on his own feet. The boots were enormously broad and enormously high, but because they were magic they had the power to grow larger or smaller to fit the person who wore them. And so they proved to be just right for his legs and feet, as though they had been made for him. Straight to the ogre's house he went, and there he found the wife crying over her butchered daughters.

"Your husband is in great danger," said Hop o' My Thumb. "He's been taken prisoner by a band of robbers who've sworn to kill him if he doesn't give them all his gold and silver. Just as they were putting a dagger to his throat, he caught sight of me and begged me to come tell you what had happened to him and have you give me all his valuables without holding anything back, or else they'll kill him in cold blood. It's so urgent that look! he gave me his seven-league boots to get here fast and also to prove to you that I'm telling the truth."

Completely terrified, the good woman at once gave him everything she had, for this ogre had not failed to be a good husband to her, in spite of the fact that he ate little children. And so Hop o' My Thumb, loaded with all the ogre's riches, returned to his father's house where he was received with great joy.

Afterword

The best-loved fairy tales in the English language are by no means English. They were first published in Paris, in 1697, under the title *Histoires ou contes du temps passé* (Stories or Tales of Times Past) and did not appear in England until 1729. Their immediate popularity with English-speaking audiences can perhaps be explained by the fact that in England itself, as the folklorist Andrew Lang pointed out nearly a hundred years ago, there were relatively few native fairy tales south of the Scottish border and east of the Welsh hills. Little Red Ridinghood, Cinderella, and the others came opportunely, therefore, and were soon naturalized. Over the years they even adopted peculiarly English names, which no translator at this late date should attempt to undo, even if the original French calls for "The Little Red Chaperon," "Cinderilla," and other equally unfamiliar locutions.

But aside from the story titles, which have acquired a life of their own independent of the French language, there is no reason why the texts should not be translated with complete accuracy. That they have not been is something of a mystery. French culture, after all, is hardly remote.

Yet none of us ever realized that Little Red Ridinghood's mother was actually baking bread that fateful morning. It seems that while she was waiting for the oven to heat up to the proper temperature she popped in a batch of flatcakes—dry, thin biscuits, or crackers—which could bake quickly without requiring much heat. In this tiny detail, imparted by the verb *cuire* (formerly "to bake bread," not merely "to bake"), listeners of long ago would have instantly recognized the sensible thriftiness of French country life.

Later, when we've reached grandmother's house, we find the door fastened with a long wooden bolt, or *bobinette*, which slides into a cavity in the door frame. A string attached to the opposite end of the bolt passes through a hole in the door. To open the door from the outside you pull the string and the bolt drops—a simple device, still in use in French villages. Yet translators have continued to get it wrong, imagining an entirely different type of latch. "Pull the bobbin, and the latch will go up," writes Robert Samber in the 1729 edition of Perrault's *Contes*, and translators ever since have done the same.

In "Bluebeard" we've been led to believe that "horsemen" come galloping into the room where the heroine is about to be murdered. But the seventeenth-century French term, *cavaliers*, means "armed gentlemen," or "soldiers of gentle birth." Hence the correct English term is "cavaliers," not "horsemen."

These and other details are clarified in Gilbert Rouger's *Contes de Perrault* (Paris, 1967), which has been one of the principal sources used in preparing this new English edition. The translation itself has been based on the Firmin-Didot facsimile of the 1697 *Histoires ou contes du temps passé*

98

(Paris, 1929). The result, it is hoped, will bring readers of English closer to the original atmosphere in which the tales were told.

The importance of these stories can hardly be overestimated. Children's literature as we know it today begins with this work. Kinship with animals, sibling rivalry, fear of desertion, fear of devourment, magical transformation, sudden riches—all the major themes are here, fully developed. Nothing quite like this remarkable book had ever appeared, and nothing since has replaced it. The Grimms' *Kinder- und Hausmärchen*, published 115 years later, added a half dozen or more tales to the canon of children's classics, including "Rapunzel" and "Rumpelstiltskin." But the popularity of "Puss in Boots," "The Sleeping Beauty," "Bluebeard," and the original "Cinderella" remained unsurpassed. The Grimms' tales are somewhat different, marked by an occasionally darker, even sinuous quality, perhaps more pleasing to adults than to children. The strength of the *Contes du temps passé* lies in its combination of sublime fantasy and absolute clarity; and all writers of children's fiction in the nineteenth and twentieth centuries, whether they have realized it or not, have been measured against this standard.

The storyteller from whom at least some of the tales were originally obtained remains anonymous. There can be little doubt that she was a woman. Possibly she was a governess in the household of Charles Perrault, the Parisian civil servant and man of letters who today is remembered not for his own works but for his having preserved the stories told by this person. She, or her prototype, appears in the first-edition frontispiece as a stout middle-aged servant, spinning beside the fire, her lips parted in speech, while three slim and elegantly attired children sit listening. Incorporated into this picture is the legend *Contes de ma mère l'Oye* (Tales of Mother Goose), which seems to serve as an alternate title for Perrault's book.

But Perrault did not invent the name Mother Goose. In seventeenth-century France all nursery tales were known as Mother Goose tales. Just why is not known. More than half a century later, the name was arbitrarily borrowed for a collection of English nursery rhymes, John Newbery's

Mother Goose's Melody. It is confusing, therefore, to refer to Perrault's stories as "Tales of Mother Goose." People nowadays think of the nursery rhymes. In any event, *Tales of Times Past* is the principal title.

And the title is apt, for this was the book that gave birth to the formula "Once upon a time. . . ." In the original French it reads *Il estoit une fois . . .* ("There was at one time . . ."), and each of the tales begins with it, except for "Puss and Boots." It was Robert Samber, the *Tales'* first English translator, who had the happy idea of inserting the word "upon." This appears to have been something new. The few genuinely English tales that have survived tend to start with "In the days of King Alfred . . ." or "In King Arthur's time. . . ." And Chaucer began many of his tales with the archaic formula "Whilom . . . ," which means "once" or "of old."

One of the virtues of Perrault's tales is that he preserved much of the original storyteller's language. To be sure, he added certain embellishments of his own. Witty remarks about domestic manners and the battle of the sexes are to be found in "The Sleeping Beauty," "Bluebeard," "Cinderella," and "Hop o' My Thumb." And "Rickety Topknot," the least familiar of the eight tales, is known to have a literary, not a folk, source. Such brittle chatter was of course more typical of the court than the nursery. And in fact, fairy tales had already become a much-appreciated amusement in elegant circles, where they were retold with such artificiality and such long-windedness that nothing at all was left of the folk style. Perrault was the first to present them in more or less their original form.

It is tempting to trim off Perrault's excess verbiage. But we wouldn't really know where to stop. Gratuitous comments and explanatory asides often appear in genuine folklore. On the other hand, we can be sure that the morals appearing in the original edition were the work of none other than Perrault himself. Their very existence is due to Perrault's anxiety about the folk origin of his material. In the dedication to Élisabeth-Charlotte d'Orléans he diffidently admits that the tales are not only folk literature but children's literature. Perhaps they will be dismissed as inelegant, foolish, and lacking in moral value. As if to compensate, he has interpreted them in versified "morals." The following sample, appended to "Little Red Ridinghood," is typical of Perrault's turn of thought.

Moral

Here you see that little children,
  Especially little girls
  Who are beautiful, well built, and pretty,
Do very badly by listening to all sorts of people,
  And it's not surprising
  That the wolf eats so many of them.
I say *the* wolf because all wolves
  Are not the same.
  There's one kind that's mild-mannered,
  Without bluster, without spite, without fury,
  Who cozily, amiably, and gently
  Follows young ladies
Into their houses, into their boudoirs,
And alas! they don't realize that these gentle wolves
Are the most dangerous wolves of all.

Notice that Perrault seems to read "Little Red Ridinghood" as an allegory of sexual awakening, an interpretation that twentieth-century Freudian critics thought they were newly discovering.

The folkloristic background of Perrault's tales has been the subject of much scholarly study. Of the eight stories, only "Little Red Ridinghood" appears to have no precedent, at least not in published form. But variants of "The Sleeping Beauty" and "Diamonds and Toads" are to be found in Boccaccio's *Decameron*; and stories at least remotely similar to "Bluebeard," "Puss in Boots," and "Hop o' My Thumb" appear in *The Arabian Nights' Entertainments* and other sources. Tales of the Cinderella type are widespread indeed, with variants recorded from China, India, and Africa.

"Rickety Topknot" is a special case. Perrault evidently adapted it from a tale in Catherine Bernard's novel of 1696, *Inès de Cardoue*.

Australia, Oceania, and the Americas are the only parts of the world that are, or were, completely free from variants of the stories that Perrault compiled. After European contact, however, the tales were learned by native peoples in these areas as well, though they were often reshaped to fit local customs. Among the Zuni of New Mexico, for example, several versions of "Cinderella" have been collected over the past hundred years. In these stories the heroine is a miserable little girl with bugs in her hair who tends a flock of turkeys. Her sisters look down on her because she refuses to help them with the housework(!). When she hears about an important ceremonial dance to be held in a nearby pueblo, she longs to go but has nothing to wear. The turkeys come to her rescue, magically producing a fine robe. And so forth.

In the Zuni variants it is interesting to note the heroine's intimate relationship with the turkeys, who talk to her and comfort her. Rapport with animals is also typical of Walt Disney's *Cinderella*. In Perrault, of course, this theme is limited to "Puss in Boots."

And what of the glass slipper? To this day there are writers infatuated with the notion that the French word *verre* ("glass") is merely a careless substitution for its homonym *vair* (a kind of fur) and that Cinderella's slipper must have originally been a fur slipper. After all, how could a slipper be made of glass?

On the other hand, why should it have been made of fur? We have no record of French footgear ever having been made of, or even lined with, fur. Yet we do find glass slippers in magical tales from Spain, Ireland, and elsewhere. It appears that the fur theory was an invention of nineteenth-century pedants, perhaps inspired by the novelist Balzac, who planted the idea in his *Études philosophiques sur Catherine de Médicis*. Perrault's first edition clearly has *verre*.

Another question that may arise is What happened to Little Red Ridinghood's rescuer? The answer is that he does not appear until the version published more than a hundred years later by the brothers Grimm.

In that story a passing hunter, who hears the wolf snoring after his double meal, comes in to investigate, slits the wolf's stomach, and frees both Little Red Ridinghood and her grandmother. But aside from this improvised ending, the Grimms' version appears to come directly or indirectly from Perrault and not from a common folk source. "Little Red Ridinghood," incidentally, is the purest, the most folkloristic, of Perrault's tales.

In addition to the eight stories in *Contes du temps passé*, Perrault collected and adapted three other folktales, entitled *Griselidis* ("Griselda"), *Peau d'âne* ("Donkey Skin"), and *Les souhaits ridicules* ("The Ridiculous Wishes," commonly known in English as "The Three Wishes"). Published in verse, these lack the vigor and spontaneity of the tales in prose. Of the three, only *Les souhaits ridicules* is well known, though not from Perrault's verse but from Mme. Leprince de Beaumont's retelling of it in her *Magasin des enfants* (1757).

For the convenience of readers who may wish to know the original titles of Perrault's eight prose tales, I here give them in full.

La belle au bois dormant ("The Sleeping Beauty in the Wood").

Le petit chaperon rouge ("The Little Red Chaperon"). Note: The chaperon was a hood covering the head, neck, and shoulders, worn by men and women during the Middle Ages; later it was reduced to a broad strip of cloth covering the top of the head and hanging down behind, though by Perrault's time even this had fallen into disuse.

La barbe bleue ("The Blue Beard").

Le maistre chat, ou le chat botté ("The Master Cat, or The Cat in Boots").

Les fées ("The Fairies").

Cendrillon, ou la petite pentoufle de verre ("Cinderilla, or the Little Glass Slipper").

Riquet à la houppe ("Riquet with the Topknot").

Le petit poucet ("The Little Thumbling"). Note: This story is not to be confused with the English fairy tale "Tom Thumb."

Through the years these eight have appeared and reappeared in literally thousands of adaptations in prose, dramatic form, verse, music, and film. We have Walter de la Mare's gardenia-scented retelling of "The Sleeping Beauty":

> Wild fruit and bushes of mistletoe flaunted in the orchards. Moss, greener than samphire and seaweed, crept over the stones. The roots of the water-lilies in the moat swelled to the girth of Asian serpents; its water shallowed; and around the castle there sprang up, and every year grew denser, an immense thorny hedge of white-thorn and briar, which completely encircled it at last with a living wall of green . . . (from Walter de la Mare, *Told Again*, Knopf, 1927).

We have James Thurber's laconic retelling of "Little Red Ridinghood" in his *Fables for Our Time*. We have Tchaikowsky's *Sleeping Beauty*, Offenbach's *Bluebeard*, Massenet's *Cendrillon*, Rossini's *Cenerentola*. We have Maurice Ravel's wistful evocation of Hop o' My Thumb, wondering what to do as he discovers that birds have eaten his trail of crumbs:

from *Ma mère l'Oye*,
piano suite for four hands,
Durand and Co., Paris, 1910

And we have Walt Disney's fairy godmother singing "Bibbidi-Bobbidi-

Boo" (a sugar-coated form of abracadabra) as she changes mice and pumpkin into a coach and six.

Such fantasies do Perrault's work no harm. If anything, they send us back to the originals with heightened respect. The tales as they were first published are swift-moving and to the point. At times they are blunt. The king was sorry over the death of his mother, we hear, "But with a beautiful wife and two children he got over it quickly." Or again, "they were not terribly wicked, though they gave much promise of being so, for even now they would bite into little children and suck their blood." At other moments, in true folk style, the narrative breaks into a chant, and we hear the strangely whimsical "Naught but sun's beams / And grass that greens," or the familiar "Grandmother, what big eyes you have!"

Despite the nuances presumably added by Perrault, the honest voice of the storyteller, older than literature, can be plainly heard. Still drawing upon the power of the unwritten word, this voice enables us to make contact not with the imaginative trappings of literary art but with the hidden sources of imagination itself.

J.B.

West Shokan, N. Y.
December 1980

Appendix/Extra Matter from the Edition of 1697

I. The Dedication

[The following dedication to Élisabeth-Charlotte d'Orléans, niece of Louis XIV, is signed with the name of Perrault's youngest child, Pierre Darmancour, evidently because Perrault was fearful of being scorned if people knew he had compiled a book of fairy tales. Perrault's own name does not appear in the first edition.]

To
Mademoiselle

Mademoiselle,

One will not find it odd that a child has been pleased to compose the tales in this collection, but one will be astonished that he has had the boldness to present it to you. But Mademoiselle, whatever the disparity between the simpleness of these narratives and the brilliance of your wit, a close inspection of these tales will show that I am not to be blamed as much as might seem at first. Each of them conceals a most sensible moral, to be discovered in greater or lesser degree according to the reader's depth of penetration. Besides, since nothing typifies a broad intellect so much as the power to reach the greatest things while at the same time stooping to the smallest, one will not be surprised if this same princess, to whom nature and breeding have made great things familiar, does not disdain to take pleasure in such bagatelles. True, these tales present a picture of what transpires in the lowliest of families, where a praiseworthy eagerness to instruct the children leads to the invention of stories lacking in wisdom, suited to those very children who themselves as yet have none. But to whom could it be more fitting to know how the people live than to those persons whom heaven has destined to be their leaders? The desire for this knowledge has carried heroes, and even heroes of your race, into huts and cottages to see for themselves, at close hand, just what transpires in particular, for it has seemed to them that this knowledge is necessary to complete their education. Be that as it may, Mademoiselle,

> Could I better choose,
> To make the fable's wonders seem possible?
> And did ever a fairy of olden times
> Give a young creature
> More gifts, and gifts more rare,
> Than nature has given to you?

With the very deepest respect, I am,
Mademoiselle,
Your Royal Highness' most humble and most obedient servant,

P. Darmancour

II. The Morals

The Sleeping Beauty

Moral

To wait for a husband / Who's rich, handsome, gallant, and kind / Is a natural enough thing, / But to wait a hundred years, sleeping all the time / —You'd never find another female / Who'd sleep so peacefully.

It seems the fable also means to tell us / That a suitable marriage bond, / Though delayed, is none the less happy, / And that nothing's lost by waiting; / But with such eagerness does the fair sex / Aspire to conjugal fidelity / That I have neither the power nor the heart / To preach this moral.

Little Red Ridinghood

Moral

Here you see that little children, / Especially little girls / Who are beautiful, well built, and pretty, / Do very badly by listening to all sorts of people, / And it's not surprising / That the wolf eats so many of them. / I say *the* wolf because all wolves / Are not the same. / There's one kind that's mild-mannered, / Without bluster, without spite, without fury, / Who cozily, amiably, and gently / Follows young ladies / Into their houses, into their boudoirs, / And alas! they don't realize that these gentle wolves / Are the most dangerous wolves of all.

Bluebeard

Moral

Curiosity, for all its charms, / Often costs many regrets; / You see a thousand examples of it every day. / With due deference to the fair sex, it's a fleeting pleasure. / Once taken, it ceases to be. / And always it costs too much.

Another Moral

Even without much of a shrewd mind / Or a knowledge of the world's learned jargon, / One may soon see that this story / Is a tale of times past; / There no longer exists such a terrible husband, / Nor one who would ask the impossible; / Even if unhappy and jealous, / He's to be seen at his wife's side, keeping quiet; / And though his beard be what color it may, / It's hard to say which of the two is master.

Puss in Boots

Moral

However great the advantage / Of enjoying a rich legacy / Coming down from father to son, / For young people in general / Ingenuity and a ready wit / Are worth more than inherited wealth.

Another Moral

If a miller's son can so swiftly / Win the heart of a princess / And have her gaze at him with languishing eyes, / It's that clothes, looks, and youth, / When it comes to inspiring tenderness, / Make a method that's not half bad.

Diamonds and Toads

Moral

Diamonds and pistoles* / Have great power over the mind; / But gentle words are mightier yet / And come at a higher price.

*A pistole is a coin worth half a doubloon.

Politeness takes effort / And needs some complaisance, / But sooner or later it has its rewards, / And often when least expected.

Cinderella

Moral

Beauty for the fair sex is a rare treasure: / One never grows tired admiring it. / But that which is named kindheartedness / Is priceless and worth even more.

It's what Cinderella's godmother allowed her to have / Through instruction and training, / And to such an extent that she made her a queen / (For such is the moral of this tale).

O beauties, this gift is worth more than being well coiffed / If you want to win a heart and succeed in your goal. / Kindheartedness is the true gift of fairies: / Without it, you can do nothing; with it, everything.

Another Moral

It's no doubt a great advantage / To have wit, courage, / Gentility, good sense, / And other similar endowments / That one receives from heaven as one's portion, / But you'll have them to no purpose, / Nor will they make your fortune, / If you've neither godfathers nor godmothers / To turn them to good account.

Rickety Topknot

Moral

What you see in this piece / Is not so much an idle tale but truth itself: / All is beauty, where there's love; / All that's loved is filled with wit.

Though an object of affection be endowed by nature / With beautiful features and lively coloring / Of a hue that art could never match, / All these gifts have less power to touch the heart / Than a single unseen charm / Revealed by love.

Hop o' My Thumb

Moral

It's by no means a problem to have many children / When they're all handsome, well built, nice and tall, / And with a shining appearance. / But if one of them is feeble or speechless, / People scorn him, jeer at him, malign him. / Yet sometimes it's this little monster / Who makes for the happiness of the whole family.

III. A Second Ending for "Hop o' My Thumb"

[After the concluding incident in which Hop o' My Thumb returns home with the ogre's riches, Perrault's text continues as follows, without interruption:]

There are many people, however, who don't agree with this last part of the story. They insist that Hop o' My Thumb never stole those things from the ogre, though in fact he didn't mind taking the boots, since the ogre only used them to run after little children. These people claim to have it on good authority, and they say they've even had food and drink at the woodcutter's house.

Well, they claim that when Hop o' My Thumb had put on the ogre's boots he went off to the king's palace, where he knew they were anxiously awaiting news from the army, which was two hundred leagues away and had been fighting a battle. Right away he went and found the king, they say, and told him that if he wanted to he would bring back news from the soldiers before the day was out.

The king promised him a huge sum of money if he could do it, and Hop o' My Thumb brought back the news that very evening.

This first mission established his reputation, and thereafter he earned as much as he wanted, for the king paid him splendid sums to carry his orders to the army. And all sorts of ladies gave him whatever he wanted for bringing news of their lovers, and that was where he made the most of all.

There were a few women who had him take letters to their husbands. But they paid so badly and it brought him so little that he didn't even bother to add up what he earned that way.

After working as a messenger for some while and saving a lot of money, he went back to his father's house, where he was welcomed with what joy you can't imagine.

He made his whole family comfortable. He paid to have new government positions created for his father and his brothers, and that's how he set them all up. And he took care of himself, in style, while he was at it.

Bibliography

Barchilon, Jacques, ed., *Perrault's Tales of Mother Goose*, The dedication manu-script of 1695 reproduced in collotype facsimile . . ., Morgan Library, New York, 1956, 2 vols. Facsimile of a manuscript version of five of Perrault's tales: *La belle au bois dormant, Le petit chaperon rouge, La barbe bleue, Le maître chat ou le chat botté,* and *Les fées.* For questions regarding the authenticity of the manuscript see Rouger (work listed below), p. lxvii.

Barchilon, Jacques, and Pettit, Henry, *The Authentic Mother Goose Fairy Tales and Nursery Rhymes,* Alan Swallow, Denver, 1960. Includes a facsimile of Robert Samber's 1729 English translation of Perrault's *Contes du temps passé* and a facsimile of John Newbery's *Mother Goose's Melody.*

Contes de Perrault, Réimpression en fac-similé des éditions de 1695 et 1697, Firmin-Didot, Paris, 1929, 2 vols. Facsimile of the tales in verse (edition of 1695) and the *Contes du temps passé* (first edition, 1697).

Johnson, A. E., trans., *Perrault's Fairy Tales*, Dover, New York, 1969. Includes the famous illustrations by Gustave Doré, originally published in 1862.

Lang, Andrew, ed., *Perrault's Popular Tales*, Oxford, 1888. French text of Perrault's tales, preceded by a folkloristic essay.

[Perrault, Charles,] *Histoires ou contes du temps passé*, Avec des moralitez, Claude Barbin, Paris, 1697. The first edition.

Rouger, Gilbert, ed., *Contes de Perrault*, Garnier Frères, Paris, 1967. The tales in verse, the tales in prose, and related matter, with introductory essays, notes, variants, glossary, and bibliographies.